the marble garden

The Marble Garden   Mark Dickinson

the marble garden

A TALE OF GOTHIC HORROR
BY
MARK DICKINSON

This is a work of Fiction.

All the characters and events Portrayed in this book are either fictitious or are used fictitiously.

The Marble Garden

ISBN: 9798588833950

Copyright 2020 Mark Dickinson

A story in the style of the Victorian Gothic

by

Mark Dickinson

All rights reserved, including the right to reproduce

This book in any form

Get more of Mark's books online!

https://www.facebook.com/MarkDickinsonPublishing/

http://www.lulu.com/spotlight/darknessembraced

https://www.amazon.com/Mark-Dickinson/e/B082RBSYBK

Published by Mark Dickinson Publishing

Dedicated to Jessica

For her endless love and support

Erika & Keegen

Proud of both of you and what you have become!

Deric Reese, Les Hernandez you guys left us way too soon. Rest in Peace my friends, you may be gone but you certainly are not forgotten.

Special Shanks to Josh Haney, Troy Vsher, William Westwater and Atomb, the vegetable violator! For the many years of fiendship, laughs and vile support. And to everyone that has followed and supported my adventures over the years!

The candles flickered upon his face as Lucian knelt beside the bed, holding Adelia's hand tightly, his wife of three short years. Her breathing labored, filling the silence of the room as she held on to the last embers of life. Tears trickled down his face as he mumbled prayers to God for her recovery or her safe passage to find peace in heaven. The Doctor had given him a grim diagnosis from the unknown malady that had brought on fever and ague, but he had held out for hope. Today though, after weeks of suffering, all optimism had failed, and her health was deteriorating quickly into a crisis of serious natures. Her fever had gotten worse, and she had slipped into unconsciousness. He did what he could to keep down the fever, but he knew what was to come. The hours ticked away, and the evening turned into the morning; he sensed the figure in black waiting patiently for her at the foot of the bed as the clock chimed three and broke the solemn silence. Her breathing ceased, her body went limp, and Death cradled her into his cold, black wings.

It had been a week since his beloved passed away, and at last, she was at rest, but Lucian could not recover from his loss. After her obsequies, he went into a deep depression. Visiting her grave daily, sometimes even staying long after dusk until the caretaker came to throw him out. *"Oi! It's time to be moving on, guv'nor. Don't ya fret those pesky grave robbers with 'ol Timmy on the watch! You can come back in the mornin'. Now be off with ya, sir!"* He said as he tipped his hat. Lucian sensed her loneliness and swore he heard her crying, but the caretaker showed no regard or sympathy for him and said, *"I be just doin' my job, sir, ain't nuthin' personal."* Just the thought of her lying in the cold, dark ground alone was enough to drive him mad. He felt guilty, leaving her in the marble garden within its bleak, lonesome solitude.

Adelia cherished nature, music, parties, laughter, long conversations, and endless stories in life. She hated silence and made sure there was some sonance to occupy the quiet. Lucian had brought her songbirds, and they resided in the solarium, filling the house with their sweet music. At night when they didn't sing, he would hum to her gentle lullaby's til she fell asleep. Westwater Manor was a large house and full of life, substantially built of stone with 80 rooms, lush gardens, and sprawling landscapes. It was now, silent and morose; Gone was the gaiety she had brought. The halls are now reticent, the parlour unwelcoming, devoid of life. The shutters had been closed, and light had not shown its warmth since she left the mortal world. The house had become as algid as the grave that she now lays in. And in the solarium, silence, Lucian neglected to feed the birds. They succumbed to hunger—their lifeless bodies filling the bottom of their cages, and he wished that their corpses were to remain as a tribute of her passing; at the offense of the servants, of course. They now sang for Adelia on the other side.

On a brisk Autumn morning, his friend Charles had stopped in to check up on him; It had been two weeks since anyone had seen him, not since the services. He and several of his friends were beginning to worry.

Charles knocked on the door, and the butler, Mr. James, had let him in. Almost immediately, he noticed how the house's atmosphere had changed from a place of warmth and life to a dark, dismal dwelling. Even Mr. James had commented on the dreariness and his concern for the master of the house. As they entered the library, Mr. James announced to Lucian, his guest, "*Master Lucian, you have a visitor.*" He then led Charles in and left.

Lucian chirped, hiding his anguish, "*Charles, my dear friend, what brings you here today?*" Charles, shocked at his appearance, replied, "*Good God, man! You look as if you've given up the ghost! Let us open these windows and let some sunlight in; its warmth will do you some good.*" He then proceeded to tear open the curtains.

Lucian cried out, "*Cease now! I wish not to bathe in its radiance!*"

Charles said sternly: "*Stop this nonsense! It'll do you some good.*"

Lucian; "*I cannot feel anything anymore. Through the kindness of cruelty, I feed on despair and woe...*"

Charles; "*What are you going on about? It would be best if you got back to living. You have responsibilities that need your attention. Now get up and get dressed; we're getting out of this house.*"

Lucian; "*Charles, I can't. I, I have prior obligations.*"

Charles; "*Lucian, the time to mourn is over; you need to let her go and move on.*"

Lucian; "*How dare you! I shall not ever forget my dear Adelia!*"

Charles; "*That's not what I meant, and you know it.*"

Lucian; "*Charles, two weeks ago, I buried my heart. Now, I care not for anything in this life but to make sure Adelia is not alone.*"

Charles; "*I do not mean to sound callous, but Adelia is gone. She is in the loving arms of the angels. She is not alone in the heavens; she is with God.*"

Lucian; "*But Charles, you don't understand; I've been to her grave, I've heard her soul weeping, I can sense her fear, her loneliness!*"

Charles; "*Do you not hear yourself? This talk of hearing her is absurd; you're suffering from psychosis! She is dead, and there is nothing more either of us can do for her. Cherish the memories that you have and let go. This obsession is not healthy.*"

Lucian; "*Come with me, to the cemetery; I'll show you! Come, we shall leave at once!*"

Lucian leapt to his feet and shouted to Mr. James that he and his guest would be leaving and was to have the carnage prepared for their journey.

The two men rode quietly to the cemetery at a steady pace, as a cold, misty drizzle blanketed them along their journey. As they approached the cemetery gates, Lucian spoke up. "*We're almost there, soon you'll hear her. You'll see, I'm not hysterical!*" Charles nodded and gave a look of concern. As they arrived at her grave, Lucian shouted to the coachmen to halt and jumped out of the carriage. The air was crisp with the scents of the season of decay. He ran to her grave and knelt, putting his ear to the ground. He looked up to Charles, who slowly made his way over, dead leaves crunching loudly under his feet. "*Look, come see and hear for yourself; she is sobbing!*" Lucian yelled while pointing to the ground where Adelia lay.

Charles knelt beside him, listening intently. He then put his ear to the ground, not hearing anything but the gentle patter of rain as it fell on the blanket of leaves. With a blank look on his face, he stood up and looked down to Lucian, and said coldly, "*I hear nothing... Nothing but the falling rain.*" Lucian replied, "*How can you not hear her? She is sobbing so loudly?*" Charles again replied, "*As I said, I hear nothing, now let us take leave of this place.*" He then turned and walked to the carriage. Lucian cried back, *"Charles, wait! Can't you hear? We can't leave her here all alone!"* Sadly and firmly, Charles spoke, *"No, Lucian, while her body is there, her soul is gone. She is not calling to you; you imagine it; now come, it is time for us to depart."* Lucian rose, slowly raising his arm and opened his mouth as if to state a rebuttal, but it had appeared he changed his mind and sauntered to the carriage, head lowered in defeat.

The two men rode back to Westwater in deafening silence, with just the clopping of the horses' hooves on the road to break the monotony; Lucian soundlessly sobbed to himself as Adelia's name quietly rolled off of his lips. After arriving back at Westwater, they gave Mr. James their wet coats, then retired to the study.

After Charles poured them each a brandy, he looked out the window in thought for a moment, then turned to Lucian, *"Lucian, my dear friend, it pains me to see you in this state of enthusiasm. While I do not subscribe to this sort of pseudoscience, belief, or whatever they call it, I know a woman, Mrs. Emma Floyd, who claims that she can contact those who have passed over. If it will help ease your mind of these fanciful delusions and put to rest this notion that Adelia is suffering, I shall contact her at once and arrange a consultation."* Lucian sat quietly for a moment then replied, *"By whatever do you mean? Can she actually speak with the deceased? I could hear Adelia's voice again?"* *"Yes, allegedly. She says she is a medium and claims the spirits speak through her."* Charles said coldly. *"Then make it so! As soon as possible! Then you will hear for yourself how she suffers."* *"As you wish,"* Charles said. He set down his brandy and walked towards the door, then looked back, *"Take care, Lucian, and I shall be in contact with you soon."* *"I am forever in your debt Charles,"* Lucian replied. Charles nodded, then turned and exited, shutting the door behind him. Lucian rose, closed the curtains, and returned to his mourning.

A few days had passed when the butler handed Lucian a letter from Charles.

My Dearest Lucian,

Arrangements have been set, and I shall be arriving tomorrow evening around eight p.m. with Mrs. Emma Floyd. She requires a round table, a pitcher of water, a writing pad, a writing utensil, and a candle. She also desires complete privacy as any interruptions could inhibit results. I have taken care of her travel expenses.

Charles

Lucian personally handled Mrs. Emma Floyd's requests in preparation for her visit, then paid a visit to Adelia's grave to inform her of his plans. As dusk approached as if by clockwork, the caretaker arrived and politely asked him to leave, he returned to Westwater and sat in the darkness to await Charles and the woman who could speak for the dead, Mrs. Emma Floyd.

It was an unusually unsettled evening. A severe storm had moved into the region, battering the manor with hail and rain. High winds caused trees to whip with a manic frenzy to and fro. As the clock struck seven, the employees were dismissed and had retired for the night. The characters gathered at the agreed-upon time, eight o'clock. They moved to the library; a table with a black table cloth was in the middle of the room. The chamber was completely dark except for a single candle in the center of the table. Arranged at the table were Lucian, Charles, Mrs. Emma Floyd at the head, her husband William holding a bell, and at her request, two more were seated to "complete the link," the butler Mr. James and the

Head house-maid Mrs. Osgood. Mrs. Emma Floyd called for silence; she laid out the rules, then asked everyone to hold hands. Her husband William began to sing a hymn as the others joined in; at its conclusion, Mrs. Emma Floyd stated that the ceremony would begin; her husband William rang the bell, as the room fell silent.

"Spirits from beyond the realm, please heed our call. We wish you no harm and ask that you come in peace." Mrs. Emma Floyd called out loudly as her husband rang the bell again. Mrs. Emma Floyd continued, *"Tonight we gather to speak with the spirit of Adelia Bell, the wife of Lucian Bell. Adelia, if you are with us, please give us a sign. Do not be afraid; we call out in peace and love; feel our healing energy. Adelia, are you with us? Please give us a sign,"* They all sat there in silence, looking around the room for the slightest movement. Mrs. Emma Floyd spoke again; *"Adelia Bell, please come to us. Your husband is worried about you. Come and ease his weary soul, speak with us. Tap on the table to alert of us your presence."* Suddenly there was a

slight tap from out of the darkness. Startled, everyone looked around the room. Lucian jumped up, crying out, *"Adelia! Is that you? Come to me, my darling!" "Please, Mr. Bell, stay seated, calm, and continue to hold hands. Do not break the circle,"* Mrs. Emma Floyd said firmly.

Once everyone had settled down, she continued to call out to Adelia; as she did, her head began to bob and weave; she mumbled undecipherable words; hummed, and acted oddly. The room instantly came to life; a chill filled the air as the curtains swayed, the chandelier began to swing, doors opened and closed. Her husband, William, asked everyone to continue to hold hands and then started to recite the lord's prayer. Mrs. Emma Floyd shot up straight and rose from her chair; the candle blew out as the voice of Adelia came from her mouth. The patrons around the table sat still in awe. *"My dearest Lucian, how I miss thee. I am so lonesome without you. Sorrow fills my heart and soul. I sit on my tomb and sense where love died, long years ago, where tears have fallen and saturated the ground. I breathe the smell of the rain; I feel the silence that surrounds me. I see the pain, the despair, the broken hearts. I see you visit every day, but I cannot feel the warmth of your touch, the tenderness of your kiss; I pray for you to take me with you and leave this solitude."* A gusting wind slammed the doors ending the communication as everything became still; then, at that moment, hysteria broke out. William struggled to light the candle as his wife collapsed to the floor with a thud. Lucian cried out to his wife, Charles, infuriated by the turn of events, began calling foul, Mr. James was distressed, pale-faced, and a gasp and Mrs. Osgood screamed, then fainted from the supernatural terror.

Lucian looked at Charles and said, *"See Charles! I told you she needs me!"* He then broke from the group, yelling, *"Adelia! Adelia! I'm coming!"* He grabbed his coat and ran out into the darkness. Once William lit the candle, he tended to his wife as Mr. James began to light the room. Charles looked around for Lucian. William was able to bring his wife around as she sat on the floor, looking dazed. Displeased by what had just occurred, Charles said to Mr. James as they helped Mrs. Osgood to her seat, "*I say! Could they have selected someone with a stronger constitution than Mrs. Osgood?"* Mrs. Osgood huffed in disapproval," *Well, I never!"* Charles replied in an apologetic tone, "*Please, Mrs. Osgood, I mean no offense.*" Mr. James smiled in response. Then Charles turned to Mrs. Emma Floyd. "*You were to convince him that his wife was at peace! Not convince him otherwise! If anything happens to Lucian, I swear it will be on your head!"* Mrs. Emma Floyd replied, "*Please, be patient. I have no power over the will of the spirits. Lucian will return in his own time, but first, we must close the circle and end the session, or else, Adelia's soul will be trapped in this realm.*"

Meanwhile, Lucian ran blindly through the black, tempestuous night to the cemetery. He reached the gates stopping for a moment, the rain falling hard upon his face as he struggled to catch his breath. He spotted the caretaker's house, rushed to the front door, and began to pound wildly.

"*Who be it?*" the caretaker asked suspiciously from inside. "*It is I, Lucian Bell! Please, you must help me. It's my wife, Adelia, she, she's still alive! I must dig her up. Please, open the door; I need your assistance!*" Lucian pleaded. The caretaker swung open the door, "*Are you bloody well trying to make a stuffed bird laugh, Mr. Bell? Your wife has been dead and buried for weeks. There ain't no hope in hell that she be alive.*" The caretaker responded harshly. Lucian grabbed the caretaker by his lapels, "*You don't understand she spoke to me! Seance! She's suffering!*" The undertaker would not tolerate any disrespect to his personal space, pushed Lucian to the ground; he landed hard, hitting his head, "*You best leave right now, Mr. Bell, before I call the Constable! And I don't ever want to see your face around here ever again!*" In a fit of rage, Lucian raised himself and grabbed a spade that was leaning on the porch, and swung it hard, hitting the caretaker square across the side of his face, sending him off the porch. His lifeless body collapsed in a heap onto the ground, blood pooling quickly in the puddle where he lay. Lucian looked down in shock at what had just transpired but had no time to waste, for Adelia had to be released from her bondage. He dragged the caretaker, struggling to get him up the steps and through the threshold, placing him on the floor inside, then closed the door behind him, grabbing the spade and fleeing towards Adelia's grave.

The awful gale raged on. Lucian was at Adelia's grave, aggressively digging until he heard a thud; he had reached her coffin! He carefully removed the final layer of dirt and mud, wiping it away with his hands, then jumped to the side as water began filling the hole, slowly opening its lid. There she lay, as she did on the day she was laid to rest, looking radiant in her wedding gown. The cold had preserved her beauty. *"I'm here, my darling; your suffering is over. At no time will I leave your side ever again. You'll be lonely, nevermore,"* he said to her lovingly. He took off his coat and wrapped it around her lifeless body and gently lifted her into his arms, climbed out of the rapidly filling repository, and marched towards the gates. They began strolling out of the marble garden back to Westwater; while he hummed to her a peaceful lullaby accompanied by the howling wind.

Back at Westwater, Mrs. Emma Floyd and company had again gathered at the table. Mr. James had extinguished all the lights. The one in the center of the table remained, and once again, they all held hands. William rang the bell, and the ceremony had resumed. Mrs. Emma Floyd spoke, *"Adelia, are you still with us? Please give us a sign of your presence."* Silence. She began to recite the lord's prayer, and the group joined in. When they finished, William rang the bell, and Mrs. Emma Floyd asked again if Adelia was in the chamber with them.

There was a movement in the room as if a strong breeze blew through an open window. Again, the curtains began to sway, items fell off the mantle-piece, several books flew across the room, and the table started to shake. Charles, suspicious, broke the chain, grabbed the candle, looked around the room, then under the table. *"Please, sir, do not break the chain,"* William whispered firmly to Charles, and he placed the candle back on the table, joining hands again with the others. "*Adelia, we come in peace, feel our loving embrace. Please come back to us.*" Mrs. Emma Floyd urgently said as her head began to oscillate. "*Your husband needs you; please come to us. Adelia, come back to us.*" The group heard a distant voice, but they could not discern a word or a breath. "*She's weak. We must end this.*" Mrs. Emma Floyd confided. "*Adelia, it is time for you to leave this earthly realm. Go to the light so that you may fi...*" Her speaking was cut off as the voice of Adelia came through. "*Lucian, where are you, my dear? I am so alone. Lucian! Lucian!*" William cut in, "*Adelia, Lucian is not here at the moment, but he needs to know that you are safe in the arms of God. Go to the light Adelia, Go to the light.*" Lightning flashed, and the shutters outside began rapping on the windows; Mrs. Emma Floyd stood up, wildly swinging her arms as if she were a marionette, then shouted, "*Where is my Lucian? I must see him! Lucian!*" Mrs. Emma Floyd began to pace around the room, frantically crying out for Lucian. Charles slammed his hands on the table and turned a look of grave reproach upon William Floyd, "*This is preposterous! This charade has gone on long enough!*" William reached across the table, pleading, "*Wait, we must end this properly. Please.*" William walked his wife back to her seat, asked everyone to hold hands again, "*Adelia, we are going to close the circle; I beg of you, go to the light so that you may find peace in the loving arms of God. We leave you now in the name of the Father, the Son, and the Holy Ghost.*" He then rang the bell three times and finished by reciting the lord's prayer. As he finished, Mrs. Emma Floyd went limp and fell face-first onto the table.

Mr. James began illuminating the chamber; William attended to his wife then asked with a concerned tone in his voice, "*Did Adelia pass over?*" Mrs. Emma Floyd replied sadly, "*No, her spirit remains in this world.*" Suddenly there was a banging on the front door and a loud creak as it opened. "*Lucian!*" Charles shouted as he ran towards the grand hall; the group quickly followed. As the group led by Charles reached the threshold, Lucian was standing in the foyer as they froze in horror at the sight. Lightning had cast his silhouette in shadow as water dripped from his clothing. He was holding his dead wife, Adelia, in his arms, her head buried in his chest. "*My God! What have you done?*" Charles asked in shock and disbelief. "*Darling, wake up Charles has come to welcome us home,*" Lucian whispered to Adelia. Adelia then slowly rose her head towards Charles, extending her pale, bluish hand in greeting. "*Charles, thank you for being such a good friend to Lucian and reuniting us. I had been ever so lonely without him...*"

THE GHOST WEATHERTON HALL

There is an old manor called Weatherton Hall that sits on top of the hill. It is large, imposing, frightening, and still. It has many tall spires that reach the sky, centered is a stained glass window that looks like an eye. It glares ominously down on the village below, where the locals know that the manor was not the place to go. As storm clouds swirl, thunder and lightning dance high overhead; it is a frightful night for the living, a night filled with dread. Inside it is garish, dusty, and gall. Spirits can be heard roaming the halls. In a chair by the fire sits an old man, who looks at old pictures and reminisces, for he is the last of his clan. He prays to God daily for his wretched soul to save. He counts the minutes till his wicked sister Lucinda returns from the grave.

A fire roared in the hearth as it crackled and spewed. It's glowing hypnotizing dance gave off an eerie vermillion hue. His eyes were glued on a portrait that hung over the mantle. A picture of a woman whose life he dismantled; she looked angry, heartless, and bold with a stare that made one's blood run cold. Lucinda was ruthless, Lucinda was cruel, and when she entered a room, the mood changed from cheer to gloom. Nothing was safe from her evil wrath; she even drowned her brother's cat in the bath. She tortured the staff, harassed her friends, and embarrassed her family, which led to her end. It was a cold and blustery December night when her brother decided to end the family's plight. He plotted and planned and prepared for the deed, to rid the family of this rotten lousy seed. He told the family of his intention, they gave him their blessing without hesitation. He looked at the calendar, then selected the date, December thirty first, he would seal her fate. It was on a night much like tonight some forty-odd years, a night that would hopefully end-all of their fears. She sat down for dinner and was in quite a fury, but her brother stayed calm, sipped his wine without worry. She complained about this, she complained about that. She complained about the way he resembled a rat. And After desert, her brother rose for a toast, a toast to his sister whom he despised the most. "*To my dear sister, whom the devil kicked out of hell, I wish you nothing but good health and stay well.*" He stood behind her chair and pulled out an ax, and when she raised her glass, he gave her several whacks. As she lay dying, before he chopped off her head, she spewed out a curse and swore she'd return from the dead. She'd come back once a year to haunt her host, she'd come back to haunt them all, and she'd be forever known as the new years eve ghost that haunts Weatherton Hall...

ABOUT THE AUTHOR

Mark Dickinson was born under a full moon on a cold January night just as the clock struck midnight. Perhaps that is the reason for his calling to the darkness. He has been a fan of horror as long as he can remember, spending many afternoons at the movie theater for the Saturday matinees, which of course, showed many classic horror movies. A self-proclaimed horror kid, he fell in love with Poe, Victorian Gothic, and the tragedies of Shakespeare. He even wrote a "Monster Musical" as a kid. He has released two Novellas, two Short Story Collections, A Children's Book, Comic Book, two Poetry Collections. Also, as a professional musician for over 30 years, he has released 30 plus albums. He is also the host of The Horror Of It All's Silent Screams at Beta Max T.V. on Roku and the web-series "The Horror Of It All," which showcases local events that go on during the month of October. He has produced, written, and acted in several films in the "Saga of the Vampire DeBlood" series. He even directed, produced, and stared in a Dramatic Reading of 'Varney the Vampyre!' If that wasn't enough, he also owns the website Horror-Punks.net. He is a volunteer at the Phelps Mansion Museum and is curator of the Death and Mourning in the 19th Century Exhibit. He resides in Binghamton, NY, with his wife and seven cats.

ALSO AVAILABLE

"Patricia", a short story in the tradition of the Victorian Gothic - Christmas Ghost Story /Winter Tale...

An eerie silence filled the air as she stood there motionless, frozen in a dark time, staring blankly into the foggy abyss. Tears stained her pale face with sadness, revenge frozen on her icy lips. Unfettered by the curse of time, she stands a silent sentinel over the grave of her beloved...

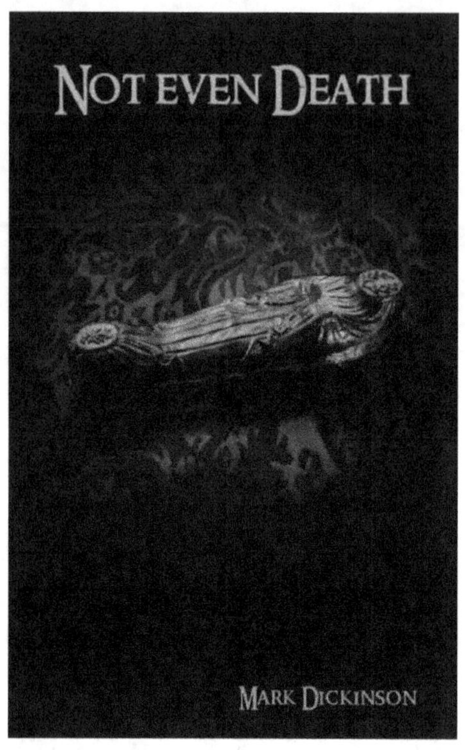

There she was, looking as alluring and radiant as the day they met. *"I'm hungry."* She stated. *"Oh, so hungry."*

"Not Even Death", A short story in the vein of the Victorian Gothic, a man recollects on meeting his wife, Azelee, their courtship, their life together, her loss and the unusual events that took place after her death regarding local superstitions.

A short story in the tradition of the Victorian Gothic

The story I'm about to share with you is about the tragic demise of a very wealthy, prominent family and the mysterious death of the family doctor of whom is at the center of the whole affair. The circumstances I shall recall to the best of my knowledge from real certainty and as they were told to me by the servant who was witness to the series of the strange events as they unfolded.

A Supernatural short story in the tradition of the Victorian Gothic... "*I discovered his diary buried under various letters, artifacts, and trinkets. As I opened the cover, I suddenly felt a chill that made the hair rise on the back of my neck, and I had the feeling that I wasn't alone anymore, the candles flickered, the drapes moved and the room filled with an eerie silence....*"